Copyright © 1985 by Shirley Hughes.
First published in Great Britain in 1985 by Walker Books Ltd.

Printed in Italy.
First U.S. edition published in 1985. 1   2   3   4   5   6   7   8   9   10

Library of Congress Cataloging in Publication Data

Hughes, Shirley.
   Noisy.
   Summary: A little girl describes the many noises that can be heard
inside and outside her house.
   1. Children's stories, English.   [1. Noise—Fiction. 2. Stories in
rhyme]   I. Title.   PZ8.3.H8665No 1985   [E]   84-12632
ISBN 0-688-04203-1

Noisy

Shirley Hughes

LOTHROP, LEE & SHEPARD BOOKS
NEW YORK

Noisy noises!
Pan lids clashing,

Dog barking,
Plate smashing,

Telephone ringing,
Baby bawling,

Midnight cats
Caterwauling,

Door slamming,

Airplane zooming,

Vacuum cleaner
Vroom-vroom-vrooming,

And if I dance and sing a tune,
Baby joins in with a saucepan and spoon.

Gentle noises . . .
Dry leaves swishing,

Falling rain,
Splashing, splishing,

Rustling trees,
Hardly stirring,

Lazy cat,
Softly purring.

Story's over,
Bedtime's come,

Crooning baby
Sucks his thumb.

All quiet, not a peep.

Everyone is fast asleep.